HENRY HAWKS
Woodland Concert

Written by
Mark Jones

HENRY HAWK'S
Woodland Concert

© 2021 Mark Jones

Illustrations © 2021 Ronice Appleby (cover illustrations)

Carina Roberts (trail map)

Design and layout: Anna Jones

British Library Cataloguing in Publication Data.
A catalogue record for this book is available from the British Library.

Published in the United Kingdom by:
Walters & Jones Publishing
(www.waltersandjones.co.uk)
in association with Trail Stories
(www.trailstories.co.uk)

First Edition: 2021

ISBN: 978-1-7398812-0-7

CONTENTS

INTRODUCTION

Penllergare Valley Woods is a secret and magical place in Wales. The acres of woodland are full of wonderful animals, amazing waterfalls, stunning lakes and magnificent trees. Once home to John Dillwyn Llewellyn and his family, the estate has a proud history of innovation and is where one of the first photographs of the moon was taken.

Come and discover Henry Hawk and his friends' woodland paradise on the edge of Swansea.

www.penllergare.org

Henry Hawk's Woodland Concert
- The Magical Trail -

Henry Hawk and his friends are planning a very special concert.
Follow our trail around Penllergare to see if you can catch a glimpse of them:
there's more information about each of the locations on this map's reverse!

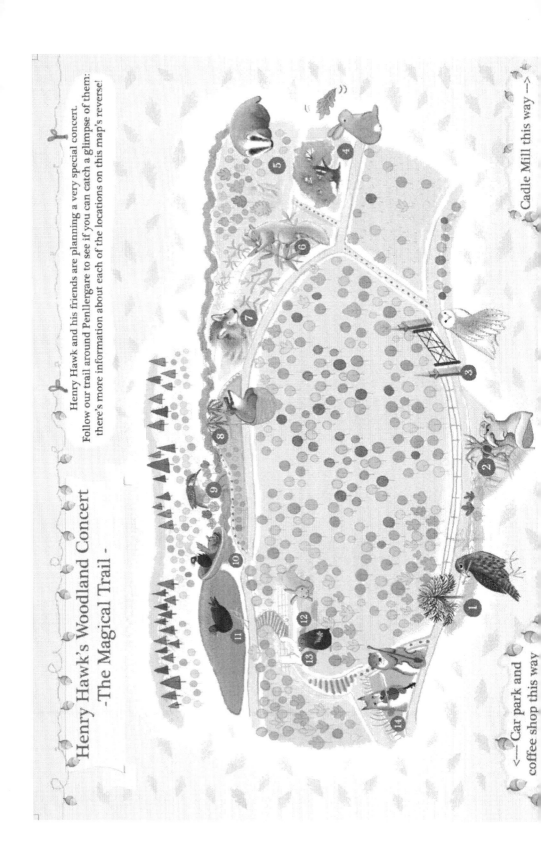

<-- Car park and
coffee shop this way

Cadle Mill this way -->

1 The Monkey Puzzle Tree
Where Henry Hawk and Hootie Owl dream up the plan for the Hawkestra Concert

2 The Goblin Tree
The home of the goblins, who might threaten to ruin the concert...

3 The Old Gates on Carriage Drive
Where Hootie asks his old friend The Man in the Moon for good weather on the night of the concert

4 The Ancient Oak Tree
Where the young rabbits gather leaves for Mosher Mole to print into promotional leaflets

5 The Tree of Ages
The home of Lemmy Badger

6 The Bamboo Forest
Where the squirrels make a basket to hoist Lemmy Badger high into the Californian Redwood trees

7 Wolf Trench
The home of the shy wolves of Penllergare

8 California Redwood Trees
Where Lemmy Badger announces the woodland concert to Penllergare Valley

9 Llewellyn Bridge
The home of the kingfishers (who make the lighting for the concert)

10 The Waterfall
Where Squizzer Squirrel and Morris Moorhen use Professor Poppleton's hoverboat to safely navigate the river

11 The Grand Lake
Where Squizzer Squirrel and Morris Moorhen deliver leaflets to animals along the banks

12 The Elephant Tree
Mosher Mole's leaflet printing station

13 The Banks - home to many creatures
The Young Rabbits deliver leaflets to all the animals who live here

14 The Grassy Glade
Where the concert takes place!

Listen to a story...Read a story...and then...Visit a story! Yes, you can actually visit the locations of all our Trail Stories! Explore woodland landscapes, lakes, rivers, hills and fields enjoying the wonders of the British countryside and discover where your favourite characters have their adventures! Hours of fun for the whole family.
www.trailstories.co.uk

Trail Stories

CHAPTER 1

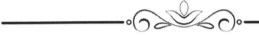

What a wonderful day! The sun is shining down from a clear blue sky and the countryside is bathed in the golden colours of autumn as the trees and hedges begin to prepare for the long winter months ahead. If I'm not mistaken, we are in South Wales and at a secret and magical place - Penllergare Valley Woods where lots of exciting adventures take place.

Settle down somewhere comfy and let me tell you how Henry the Hawk staged a never to be forgotten concert for all the woodland creatures.

Henry the Hawk was talking to Hootie the Owl. It was late in the afternoon and the sun was a large orange fiery glow as it began to set in the west. This was Henry and Hootie's favourite time of the day. They were perched at the very top of a tall monkey puzzle tree.

'D'you know,' began Hootie, 'this is the third tallest monkey puzzle tree in the United Kingdom?'

Hootie, being an owl, had a reputation for being the wisest creature that lived in the wooded valley.

Henry Hawk did not reply. His mind was far away thinking about his grand idea.

'A penny for your thoughts, Henry,' said Hootie, who was slightly offended at being ignored.

Henry turned his head to look directly at Hootie. His big beak and flashing eyes made him quite intimidating to look at and many of the woodland creatures were slightly scared of him. However, Henry was quite a gentle creature and his biggest passion was music.

'A woodland concert,' muttered Henry. 'I'm going to conduct my Hawkestra and the concert will be the biggest and best that Penllergare has ever seen. It will be the perfect end to the autumn and will cheer up all the animals who have to face the hard winter months ahead.'

This was quite a long speech for Henry. Hootie was very impressed and swivelled his head right around as only owls can do.

'I organised a barn dance once,' recalled Hootie. 'We had a bit of trouble from the wild boars and a crazy hare called Hendricks turned up with an electric guitar. Some of the animals still talk about that night. I was lucky that Lemmy Badger and his pals together with Detective Dixon Vole, Sweeney Squirrel and the Squirrel Squad were on hand to keep law and order. That Hendricks Hare made the audience go wild!'

Hootie realised he was rambling rather and returned to the matter in hand.

'A woodland concert – what a marvellous idea! I will help you plan the event. Indeed, I can see that it will be a wonderful end to the autumn!' exclaimed Hootie.

As the sun set and a full moon rose in the dark velvet night sky, and as thousands of twinkling stars appeared as distant pin-pricks of light, Hootie and Henry made their plans and discussed the idea long into the night.

CHAPTER 2

Hootie the Owl was an expert at planning events. His first task the next morning was to organise the publicity. It would not be a very good concert if nobody came because they didn't know about it.

Hootie decided to visit Mosher Mole. It was always difficult to know where to find Mosher as most of the time he lived in underground tunnels, and he was always digging new ones! However, Hootie had devised an easy way to make contact with the mole. He swooped down from the sky and landed on a grassy area in the shade of a huge oak tree. He then began stomping his claws up and down on the grass in a rhythmic pattern. He went:

Stomp, stomp ... Stomp, stomp, stomp ... Tap, stomp, tap, tap ... Tap.

Hootie was using Morse Code and spelling out the letters that made up the word MOLE.

Far below the ground, Mosher Mole pricked up his ears. He had very good hearing, which made up for his poor eyesight. Hearing Hootie's message, Mosher started scrabbling away at the earth with his powerful front paws.

Hootie waited patiently by the ancient oak tree.

Suddenly he heard a shuffling, rumbling sort of noise and a mound of fresh brown earth began to appear close by him. And just as suddenly, Mosher Mole's head popped up from the mound of earth. The little mammal blinked in he sunlight. To help him see, he had a pair of spectacles perched on the end of his pointy nose.

'Hello Mosher,' Hootie greeted the mole. 'Thank you for coming so quickly. I need your help. Henry Hawk is organising an autumn concert and we need to promote it. You are the best printer in the woodland and we would like you to print and distribute details of the event to all the woodland creatures.'

The mole replied in his slow deliberate voice, 'That would be my pleasure. Just leave it with me.'

Some time later, Mosher Mole was standing on top of his fresh mound of earth. Gathered all around him were dozens of young rabbits.

'Now then,' began Mosher, 'I want all you rabbits to collect as many oak leaves as you can from the Ancient Oak Tree over there and then bring them along to the Elephant Tree.'

The young rabbits scampered off, all chatting excitedly to one another. Mosher, meanwhile, flexed his front paws and started digging a new tunnel. He had a very good sense of direction and very soon arrived at the base of the Elephant Tree. This was another strange tree that had been in Penllergare for as long as any of the animals could remember. From a distance, the tree looked just like an elephant with a long trunk.

Mosher Mole waited patiently for the young rabbits to arrive with the oak leaves.

Soon there was a scurrying sound as the first rabbits began to arrive. Mosher instructed the rabbits to make a pile of the golden oak leaves. The mole, being a master printer, had already carved a stamp out of an old piece of wood. The stamp said:

'Henry Hawk presents a
woodland concert tomorrow
night in the grassy glade.
All are welcome to celebrate the
end of autumn.'

The mole had mixed some freshly dug earth with water from the nearby lake and now had a bucket full of sticky mud. He rubbed the stamp in the mud and then placed the stamp on an oak leaf. As if by magic, words appeared on the leaf. Satisfied that this was fine, Mosher spent the next few hours printing up what he liked to call 'promotional leaf-lets'.

When he had printed several hundred leaf-lets, he summoned all the young rabbits again, who were only too eager to help. Each rabbit took a handful of leaf-lets and set off along all the paths through the woodland to deliver them to all the creatures. They left a leaf-let in every nook and cranny. There were lots of banks where tree roots and rocks hid the entrances to the homes of many creatures.

CHAPTER 3

While Mosher was busy printing his leaf-lets, Hootie had been talking to another of his bird friends, Woodville the Wood Pigeon.

Woodville's ancestors had played important roles as carrier-pigeons during the Second World War carrying vital messages behind enemy lines. Woodville was very proud of this and in his own way, liked to think he was carrying on the family tradition. Together with Hootie, he had invented a clever way to communicate with all the birds that lived in the Penllergare Valley Woods. They called their communication a 'tree-mail'.

Hootie told Woodville about the planned concert and asked Woodville to start spreading the word. Woodville immediately flew off to the tallest trees in the valley. These were huge California Redwood trees.

The pigeon perched himself at the very top of the very tallest California Redwood. Then, he cleared his throat and started to sing and warble his important announcement across the woods.

Soon other birds flying nearby and others in their nests heard Woodville's message. In turn, they too began to pass on the details and soon the whole of Penllergare Valley Woods resounded to the sounds of hundreds of bird calls as Woodville's tree-mail was passed on.

Now, Hootie was a meticulous bird and did not like leaving anything to chance. So far he had arranged a leaf-let drop and a tree-mail but he was not satisfied. He could not be sure that all the creatures knew about the concert.

Hootie flew deep into the woods and visited the home of Lemmy Badger. The entrance to Lemmy's set was to be found beneath the roots of the Tree of Ages. This was a tree which had been a part of the woodland landscape for as long as any creature could remember.

Hootie knocked on Lemmy's front door with his beak and waited patiently.

After a few moments, an old wooden door opened and Lemmy Badger grunted a greeting to Hootie. Lemmy Badger was also a very wise animal and could be very fierce if needed. All the woodland creatures respected the badger and had elected him as both a woodland police constable and the Penllergare Town Crier.

Hootie explained all about the planned concert and asked Lemmy whether he would perform an announcement.

'Of course, of course, old chap,' grunted the badger. 'Now let me just put on my red town crier's coat, my tricorn hat and find my bell.'

The badger disappeared inside his set and emerged again soon after dressed in his town crier outfit. He looked very smart and very important.

Hootie explained that the birds had already sent out a tree-mail. Lemmy suggested that he too should find a high place from which to make his announcement.

'The highest place in Penllergare Valley Woods is at the top of the California Redwoods,' stated Hootie.

'That's as maybe,' replied Lemmy. 'But I'm a big old badger and I don't have wings. How am I going to get all the way to the top of such a tall tree?'

'You leave that to me,' said Hootie. 'I'll meet you at the California Redwoods in an hour's time.'

With that, Hootie flew off to meet Squizzer Squirrel.

Squizzer was another clever animal and his cousin was Sweeney Squirrel who worked with the famous woodland detective, Dixon Vole.

Hootie explained that he had a couple of jobs for Squizzer. Firstly, they had to devise a way to get Lemmy Badger up to the top of the California Redwood trees and then down again.

'Leave it to me,' ordered Squizzer. The squirrel scampered off into the trees and soon returned with a dozen other squirrels.

Having explained his idea to them, the squirrels set off for the bamboo forest. This is what they called the area in Penllergare Valley Woods where hundreds of bamboo trees grew.

Some of the squirrels collected bamboo stalks, whilst others collected lots of soft green moss and feathery ferns.

They then set about their work and had soon made a big bamboo basket. They lined this with the moss and ferns so that it was nice and comfortable.

The squirrels carried the basket to the California Redwood trees where they met Lemmy Badger and Hootie Owl. They then tied lengths of vine together and knotted several lengths to the basket.

'Right, climb into the basket, Mr Town Crier,' instructed Squizzer Squirrel.

'Are you sure it's safe?' asked the badger rather nervously.

'Of course it is. Trust us squirrels,' assured Squizzer.

Lemmy nervously climbed into the bamboo basket. Squizzer then took one end of a vine and several other squirrels did the same. They raced right to the top of the trees with the vines and dropped them over the highest branch.

'COME ON EVERYONE,' shouted Squizzer down to the squirrels still on the woodland floor.

The remaining squirrels quickly ran up the tree. All the squirrels – and there were dozens of them now – grabbed hold of the vines and began to pull. The rope vines creaked under the weight of the badger.

The bamboo basket containing the badger began to lift into the air.

'Oooh, er!' exclaimed Lemmy, as he became airborne.

In next to no time, Lemmy was at the top of the tree. He carefully stood up in his basket and making sure he was well balanced, began to ring his bell. The basket shook a little as he did this, but the squirrels held on tight to the vine ropes.

The bell rang out loud and clear across the valley.

'OYEZ! OYEZ! OYEZ!' cried Lemmy Badger at the top of his voice. 'NOW HEAR THIS. TOMORROW EVENING AT DUSK, HENRY HAWK WILL BE CONDUCTING HIS HAWKESTRA IN A GRAND WOODLAND CONCERT. EVERYONE IS INVITED TO THIS AUTUMNAL SPECTACULAR. GOD SAVE THE QUEEN!'

Lemmy's words rang true and clear across the woodland valley. There was no doubt that every creature would have heard the announcement.

The squirrels carefully worked to gently lower the bamboo basket, and Lemmy was immediately thankful when he safely landed back on the ground.

'Right, that's me done,' he gruffly uttered in relief. 'I'll see you all at the concert tomorrow.'

Hootie thanked all the squirrels for their help and

then turned to Squizzer. 'I have one more important job for you, Squizzer. I believe that all the woodland animals and birds now know about the concert, but I'm not so sure about the riverbank creatures. As you are an expert sailor, could I ask you to deliver leaf-lets along the riverbank?'

'Leave it to me,' replied Squizzer. 'It will be a pleasure.' With that, Squizzer scampered off to find his sailing companion, Morris Moorhen.

With the publicity taken care of, Hootie turned his mind to other plans he had to make. He decided that the next person he had to visit was Professor Poppleton.

CHAPTER 4

The Professor lived in an old observatory on the edge of the woodland. The observatory had been built in the 1850s by a Welsh gentleman called John Dillwyn Llewelyn. Mr Llewellyn's daughter had taken one of the first ever photographs of the moon from the observatory and it was for this reason that Professor Poppleton had bought the old building as he was constructing his own rocket ship in which he planned to travel to the moon.

Now Professor Poppleton was a very clever scientist and not long after he had arrived at Penllergare he had realised it was a magical place. He had soon become friends with many of the woodland creatures and liked to help them in any way he could.

Hootie knocked on the door of the observatory. The Professor quickly answered and enthusiastically greeted his old friend. The Professor was wearing a white lab coat. He had several pairs of glasses perched on his nose and his white hair was standing on end as if he had just had an electric shock!

'Hootie, my dear friend, how nice to see you,' enthused the Professor. 'Come in, come in.'

Hootie flew inside. The interior of the observatory was full of strange machines. Some were ticking, some were clicking, some were whirring, some were clanking and others were even gurgling! It was like a mechanical performance!

Hootie told Professor Poppleton all about the planned concert.

'How wonderful, wonderful!' enthused the Professor. 'I have a new invention I'd love to try out. It's a portable recording studio. I will record the concert so that the creatures can each have a recording to play for themselves during the long, dark winter months. It will help keep them cheerful until the spring arrives.'

CHAPTER 5

Squizzer Squirrel found his friend Morris Moorhen bobbing along on the Grand Lake.

'Come on Morris, we've work to do,' called Squizzer.

The two friends strode along the banks of the lake until they arrived at a little boathouse.

Taking a small key that they kept hidden beneath a pile of pebbles, Squizzer unlocked the padlock on the boathouse door. Inside, a little sailing boat bobbed up and down on the water. It had a red sail and was kept in ship-shape order by the two creatures. They liked nothing better than to sail down the lake with a gentle breeze behind them. However, on this occasion they could not rely on the wind as they had an important task to perform.

Moored next to the sailing boat was, believe it or not, a hoverboat! This machine was another of Professor Poppleton's inventions and he had asked Squizzer Squirrel to be his chief test pilot. Of course, Squizzer had jumped at the chance.

The two friends climbed on board the hoverboat and then lifted a sack on board containing the promotional leaf-lets.

Squizzer pressed a green button on the control panel and the hoverboat's engine purred into life.

The engine was very quiet, more like a hum than a roar. Professor Poppleton had purposely designed it that way as he did not think the woodland creatures should be disturbed by loud noises and nor should the peacefulness of Penllergare Valley Woods be broken.

The hoverboat purred along the Grand Lake. Every now and then Squizzer would steer towards the bank and Morris would deliver a leaf-let to a lake dwelling creature. Many of these were ducks, but there were also his family of moorhens, kingfishers, otters, water voles, water rats, toads and frogs to name but a few.

Squizzer and Morris had soon delivered leaf-lets to all the lake dwelling creatures.

Now came their next challenge. At the end of the lake was a waterfall that flowed into the river which snaked its way through the woodland valley. They would not have been able to navigate the waterfall in their sailing boat but the hoverboat made the task a bit easier. However, it was still a dangerous manoeuvre and only skilled sailors like Squizzer and Morris could have managed it.

Squizzer positioned the hoverboat so that it was pointing at the centre of the waterfall. He did not need to use any power, the current moved the craft forward. Slowly but surely the vessel headed toward the edge of the lake and then suddenly plunged over the waterfall.

Squizzer and Morris held on tight but they need not have worried. Professor Poppleton's invention worked very well. The hoverboat landed on the river below with a gentle plopping splash.

The two sailors then set off along the winding river delivering the leaf-lets announcing the grand concert to all the riverbank dwellers.

CHAPTER 6

While Squizzer and Morris travelled down the river, Hootie was still busy with his plans. He had sent a team of rabbits and squirrels to collect as many acorn cups as they could. The woodland creatures had a secret way of making acorn lights.

Some of the shyest birds that lived in Penllergare Valley Woods were the kingfishers. They tended to keep themselves to themselves and did not like to mix with the other animals. However, Hootie knew they were very clever and intelligent birds and he had persuaded them to be in charge of the concert lighting.

The grassy glade was going to be lit by strings of acorn lights.

Hootie needed one more ingredient. He flew across the valley to visit Mr Honeyman, the beekeeper.

Mr Honeyman was tending his beehives when Hootie swooped down. 'Hello, Hootie,' greeted the beekeeper. 'How nice to see you. What can I do for you on this fine day?'

Hootie told Mr Honeyman about the concert and asked the beekeeper for some of his special beeswax.

The beekeeper was more than happy to let the owl have some of the wax. Hootie thanked him graciously and flew off to meet the kingfishers.

The kingfishers lived on their own in nests they had made beneath an old bridge that crossed the river deep in the woodland. The bridge was known as Llewelyn Bridge to the residents of Penllergare Valley Woods.

Hootie called out to the shy birds and left the special beeswax beside the hundreds of acorn cups on the riverbank. He knew the kingfishers would get to work creating the acorn lights.

It was almost dark now and Hootie was very tired. This was unusual as he was normally a night-time creature but he had worked hard during the daylight hours today and was quite weary now. Before he went to bed, he had one more task to perform.

Hootie flew down to the big gates that crossed the old Carriage Drive which ran through the woods. He perched on one of the gates and called out to The Man In The Moon, who was an old friend.

The Man In The Moon could control the weather and Hootie wanted to make sure that it would be fine for the concert tomorrow night.

Some grey clouds floated across the moon.

Hootie called out to the moon again. Suddenly, a face began to appear on the moon.

'Hello my old friend,' responded The Man In The Moon. His voice softly echoed across the sky. 'And what can I do for you?'

Hootie explained about the concert and then asked The Man In The Moon if he would arrange for the weather to be fine.

'Yes, my old friend, I think I can help,' he softly replied. 'All you have to do is to place the Moonjewels in a circle on the ground tonight and say the magic rhyme.'

And with these words echoing softly across the land, The Man In The Moon's face gently faded away.

Hootie knew exactly what to do. When he had held his barn dance, The Man In The Moon had told him to collect some magic Moonjewel stones from secret places all around the world. By placing these magic stones in a circle and reciting the magic rhyme, you could summon the Moonwind – a special breeze that blows away any rain.

The owl flew back to his home which was in an old timbered barn on a farm on the very edge of the valley. The farmer did not use this barn very often and so had never seen the special Moonjewel stones that Hootie had placed in a circle on the floor of the barn.

Hootie flew down from his perch in the roof of the barn and landed in the centre of the Moonjewel circle. Concentrating hard, he recited the magical rhyme:

Moonjewels, Moonjewels,
Hear these words loud and clear.
Please blow away the big black
clouds,
And make the rain disappear.

Having finished his rhyme Hootie flew back up to his favourite beam for a good night's sleep. It had been a long day. He hoped the Moonwind would blow away any rain and that the concert tomorrow would be a great success.

Hootie wriggled around a bit to find the most comfortable spot. He tucked his wings in contentedly and then gave a satisfied sigh. Soon after he gently dropped off to sleep.

CHAPTER 7

The next day dawned with another clear blue sky and as the sun rose, the wooded valley began to warm up. It was a marvellous day for a concert.

Hootie stretched his wings and then flew through the doors of his barn and headed towards the glade where the concert was to take place.

When he arrived he found the glade a hive of activity. The kingfishers had strung hundreds of acorn lamps together which they had hung from the trees that surrounded the area on three sides.

The hedgehog family had set up a stall ready to sell the concert programmes, which Mosher Mole and his team were busy printing in the shade of the Elephant Tree.

In another corner the fox family had set up their refreshments area. They had been really busy making their very popular blackberry autumn cordial drink. They were up very early collecting fresh dew water from the surrounding meadows and into this water they crushed the blackberries and some other secret ingredients which had also been freshly picked that morning.

Even the chickens had turned up with their chuck wagon. The chickens lived in the farmyard next to Hootie's barn but considered themselves part of the Penllergare family. They were going to sell honey fudge which they made with the honey from Mr Honeyman's bees and the cream from the farm.

At the far end of the glade, the wild boars had erected a stage made from bales of straw and old tree trunks. The wild boars were very strong animals and they were on their best behaviour. Lemmy Badger had promised them front row seats if they behaved themselves.

Henry Hawk was busy organising his Hawkestra. There were dozens of animals included. Most of them played instruments but there were also several singers. Firstly there were the small nuthatches. These tiny birds were excellent singers and together with the wagtails made up the feathered choristers.

Henry Hawk was also feeling very pleased with himself. The oldest animals living in Penllergare Valley Woods were the ancient wolves. There were not many wolves left in the woods these days but a small family lived in a dark area of the woodland which the creatures knew as The Wolf Trench. Henry had persuaded the wolves to join his orchestra.

They were good singers and decided to call themselves The Howling Wolves.

Hootie could see that all was progressing well. There was not much more he could do now so he flew off to see Lemmy Badger.

However, he had not flown far when he spotted down below two small figures scurrying along a woodland path. He swooped down to see who they were.

'Oh, Hootie, it's good to see you,' smiled Dixon Vole. Hootie was pleased to see the famous woodland detective and his trusty sidekick, Sweeney Squirrel.

'Good morning, Detective,' responded Hootie. 'You seem to be in a great hurry this morning.'

'We've had a tip-off,' reported Sweeney, in a grim voice. 'The Goblins are planning to spoil the concert tonight. We're off to their hidey-hole to pay them a visit and if necessary, arrest them.'

'That's typical of the Goblins,' replied Hootie. 'They're the only creatures in the whole of Penllergare who are spiteful. You'll need some help. I've got an idea – let's meet at the Goblin Tree in ten minutes.'

With that, Hootie took off and flew swiftly back to the glade. He landed next to the pack of wild boars and approached their leader, whose name was Ozz Boar. The owl explained that the Goblins were up to mischief and threatened to spoil the concert.

Ozz Boar cottoned on very quickly. 'Leave it to us, Hootie,' he said, reassuringly. 'We'll sort those Goblins out.'

The leader of the wild boars addressed his fellow boars. 'Come on chaps. We must sort out the Goblins. They're not going to spoil this concert. They need a jolly good biff on their noses.'

The wild boars got rather excited at this point. 'FIGHT, FIGHT, FIGHT! they all shouted as they set off for the Goblin Tree like a bunch of rowdy football supporters.

Hootie smiled to himself. The Goblins were going to be in for a nasty surprise. That would teach them for being spiteful.

CHAPTER 8

Hootie knew that the Goblins did not like nice things, especially music. They lived behind the roots of an ancient tree which was perched on top of a rocky cliff face. The roots of the tree could be seen holding on to the cliff face. It really did look as though the Goblin Tree could topple over at any moment.

The wild boars came stomping up to the Goblin Tree. Dixon Vole winced at the noise they were making. He had been hoping to take the Goblins by surprise but now there was no chance of this.

Ozz Boar noticed the detective and his sergeant standing quietly beneath a beech tree.

'Morning Detective,' said Ozz Boar, 'You leave this to us. We can't have you getting your paws dirty.'

Before the woodland detective could reply, Ozz Boar stuck his head out so that his sharp tusks pointed forward. 'CHARGE!' he roared at the top of his voice.

All the boars stuck their heads down and charged at the Goblin Tree. The ancient tree shook under the impact of a dozen wild boars head-butting it together.

Goblins popped out from behind the roots. They had been taken completely by surprise and looked dazed.

'You'd dare to spoil our concert would you?' roared Ozz Boar. 'Let's get 'em chaps.'

There was quite a scuffle as the wild boars biffed the Goblins on their ugly noses.

It was all over quite quickly. The Goblins retreated behind the roots of their tree and promised not to come out again until after the concert was over.

Satisfied with their work, the wild boars set off back towards the glade, thumping each other on the back and congratulating each other for successfully dealing with the problem.

Dixon Vole made a note in his case book and turned to Sweeney Squirrel. 'Well, that's sorted those Goblins out. Let's go and get some lunch.'

CHAPTER 9

The afternoon wore on and before long the sun began to set and the moon began to rise. A wonderful twilight settled over he valley. In the glade, creatures began to arrive for the concert. The hedgehogs were busy selling programmes, the fox family's refreshment table was doing a roaring trade and the chickens were selling bags of creamy honey fudge from their chuck wagon.

All the acorn lamps had been lit and the special beeswax burned with a soft glow. Hundreds of twinkling lights hung from the tree branches giving the glade a magical feel.

The musicians were tuning up. Henry Hawk had written a special piece of music that his Hawkestra were going to play. It was called, 'A Secret and Magical Place'.

Professor Poppleton had arrived with his portable recording studio. He had set this up at the back of the glade. He sat at a complicated looking control panel. This was covered in flashing lights and dozens of switches and levers. On top of the control panel, two enormous reels of recording tape were whirring around. It looked like he was in the middle of his own night club.

Soon it was time for the concert to start. The woodland glade was packed. You could not have squeezed in another creature. To control the audience a group of badgers were acting as bouncers. However, there was no sign of trouble. Dixon Vole, Sweeney Squirrel and the Squirrel Squad were on standby, just in case the Goblins turned up.

Lemmy Badger, dressed in his Town Crier's outfit stood in front of the expectant crowd. He held up a paw and the audience fell silent.

'Fellow Penllergare residents,' he began, 'welcome to this very special woodland concert. This event is to celebrate the wonderful year we have had and to help us face the harsh winter months ahead. So enjoy yourselves as I now have great pleasure in introducing Henry Hawk and his magnificent Hawkestra!'

The audience clapped and cheered in anticipation of the spectacle about to unfold. Henry Hawk picked up his baton. A hush fell over the glade. Henry brought his baton down and his Hawkestra began to play.

It was a wonderful sound and the sweet music echoed around the valley. The nuthatch and wagtail choristers sang their little hearts out.

Bert Badger thumped away on his bass drum whilst his cousin Betty Badger played percussion.

The brass section, which was made up of squirrels and rabbits, were parping away on their trumpets, saxophones, trombones and cornets.

The string section was made up from otters, ferrets, foxes and a host of other creatures. Their violins, violas and cellos created the most glorious melody and the combined sounds created music that bathed the landscape far and wide.

And then there were the howling wolves adding their own unique sound.

It truly was a marvellous concert.

Professor Poppleton's mobile studio was recording every note and over the following days every creature would be given a recording they could listen to during the winter months.

And there we must leave them. All the Penllergare creatures are having a wonderful time and although they don't know you have been sharing their adventure, I'm sure that if they did, they would invite you to Penllergare to see for yourself what a magical place it is.

Who knows, if you look very carefully you might just catch a glimpse of Henry Hawk, Hootie Owl, Dixon Vole or Squizzer Squirrel.

ABOUT THE AUTHOR

Mark Jones was taught how to write a television script by Gerry Anderson, the legendary producer of *Thunderbirds, Captain Scarlet, UFO* and other world famous sci-fi television series. Mark worked as an advisor to Anderson in the early 1980s during the production of *Terrahawks*, negotiating promotional and licensing agreements. Mark co-wrote and co-produced his first television pilot, *Starwatch* in 1984, which featured *Doctor Who* and *Worzel Gummidge* star, Jon Pertwee and which was considered by the BBC as a possible Saturday evening replacement *for Doctor Who.*

Over the years he has been involved in many television projects producing the pilot of *Odd Adventures,* which despite being for young children, employed high production values, the special effects and model work being undertaken by the team that had worked on the feature films *Alien, Flash Gordon* and *Outland.* This was followed by producing *Scott Saunders In Outer Space* with Sir Patrick Moore, *The Twitchies* with Gary Wilmot, *Merlin's Memories* and *Crudney & Co,* to name but a few.

Mark followed a career in marketing and advertising during which he wrote hundreds of creative proposals in answer to client briefs and pitched these ideas in boardrooms across the UK and across a variety of industries. The first television commercial he worked on was directed by Sir Alan Parker.

Mark is passionate about music and has contributed to the *Guinness and Virgin Encyclopaedias of Popular Music.* He is also a television historian and penned a locally best selling book on the hundreds of film and television locations in the area that is now referred to as *Midsomer Murders* country – the Chilterns and Thames Valley.

A recent project has seen Mark create *Time to Sleep Stories*. These are audio stories for children specifically designed to help them relax at bedtime. The charming tales use simple breathing techniques which, when combined with a child's imagination, can have an astonishingly calming effect on lively young minds. November 2020 saw these audio stories become available to a worldwide audience via the launch of a new app.

During 2018 Mark completed work on two Doctor Who related books, *Lethbridge-Stewart 'United in Blood'* and the *Lethbridge-Stewart Quiz Book*. Two new children's books, *Captain Cutlass And His Rocket Ship'* and *The Adventures of Dixon Vole: Woodland Detective* were also published and both stories have already received interest form animation production companies.

As a busy writer, Mark is always working on new scripts and stories. He is currently developing a new sci-fi series, *L.O.N.D.O.N.* (influenced by his work with Gerry Anderson) which is under consideration by several broadcasters together with writing and producing new tales for Time To Sleep Stories and Trail Stories.

ABOUT THE ILLUSTRATORS

RONICE APPLEBY

Ronice Appleby is an artist and illustrator, specialising in analogue illustration. Her style aims to construe and blend realistic details with fantastical themes and subjects through a traditionally illustrative aesthetic. She has always drawn inspiration from the imaginative and magical world of children's literature, which she also uses to depict elements that promote nostalgia and speaks to audiences of all ages.

Ronice studied at the University for the Creative Arts in Surrey, where she completed a Bachelors Degree in illustration. Since graduating, she has produced her own range of greetings cards, publications and merchandise, as well as working within children's narratives. Ronice's most recent venture is for Time to Sleep Stories. Here we see these charming and imaginative tales come to life through her playful imagery and meticulous eye for detail.

CARINA ROBERTS

Carina is an artist and illustrator, specialising in children's illustration for books and greetings cards. A love of the natural world inspires everything that Carina does - she was particularly excited to work on her first commission for the National Trust recently.

Carina spent her childhood drawing, reading and exploring outdoors, looking for animals to befriend. A degree in illustration at UWTSD (previously Swansea

Metropolitan University) opened up a world of possibilities for Carina, nurturing the development of the beloved gouache and layered coloured pencil technique she uses to this day. A love of books solidified the inspiration Carina found in the written word and won her the Dylan Thomas Art & Design Award in 2014, just before she graduated.

Life as an illustrator also allows Carina a variety of valuable opportunities to leave her desk and work with her audience directly- assisting at nursery and forest school settings for children has allowed Carina to share her passions for the natural world as well as helping a new generation to develop their creative and visual communication skills.

Carina loves exploring the coastlines, forests and countryside of her home in Wales, regularly going for walks in the nearby Penllergare Valley Woods to find inspiration for her next project. She always keeps an eye out for Henry Hawk and his friends!

Henry Hawk's Woodland Concert is available as an exciting audio story on the Trail Stories app.

Trail Stories is available to download from the Google and Apple App Stores

You may also like the Time to Sleep Stories app.

Time to Sleep Stories is also available to download from the Goggle and Apple App Stores.

Time to Sleep Stories are wonderfully relaxing, gentle bedtime tales for children featuring calming narration, dreamy music and tranquil sound effects.

Over 25 stories are available to download on the app and a brand new unique story is added every month. Taking out a subscription (just £0.99 per month) will mean having your own magical library on your chosen device.

> *'This app really helped to relax my children at bedtime and they enjoy the stories. I use it every night.'* Amira Jones

> *'I have always struggled to get my daughter to sleep at night time, being a very hyper child who does not settle for bed time. However, since using these stories in her bed time routine she settles down with ease. She looks forward to hearing a story every night.'* Lisa Thomas